P9-DGN-496

WITHDRAWN
MUSSER PUBLIC Library

MUSSER PUBLIC LIBRARY
MUSCATINE, IA 52761

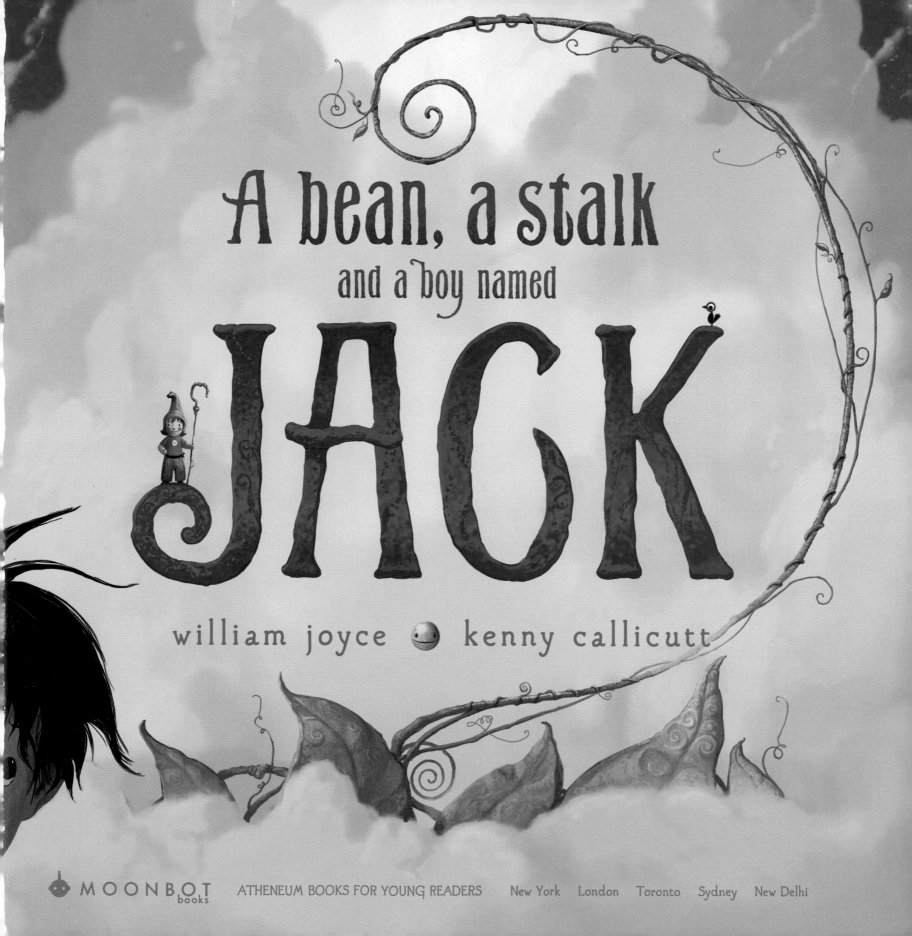

A bean, a stalk
and a boy named
JACK

william joyce • kenny callicutt

MOONBOT books   ATHENEUM BOOKS FOR YOUNG READERS   New York   London   Toronto   Sydney   New Delhi

3 0088 00054 7017

OCT 2 0 2014

Once upon a time
there was a smallish green bean,
regular as they come.

The last one outta the pod.

MUSSER PUBLIC LIBRARY
MUSCATINE, IA 52761

Did it look like a bean that would make a difference?

Did it look like a bean of destiny?
HARDLY!

But, you know . . . things can happen.

There was also a smallish kid
with the smallish name of Jack.
He had a smallish mom, a smallish dad,
a smallish cow, and a smallish farm.

That's about it. No great shakes.

But like I said . . . *things* can happen.

Or rather they didn't.

As in, it didn't rain for so long
that the crops dried up.
And the wells dried up,
and the rivers and the lakes
and the moats and the birdbaths.

So the people were thirsty,
the fish were uncomfortable,
the birds were unbathed,
and the king's royal pinky
had become stinky.

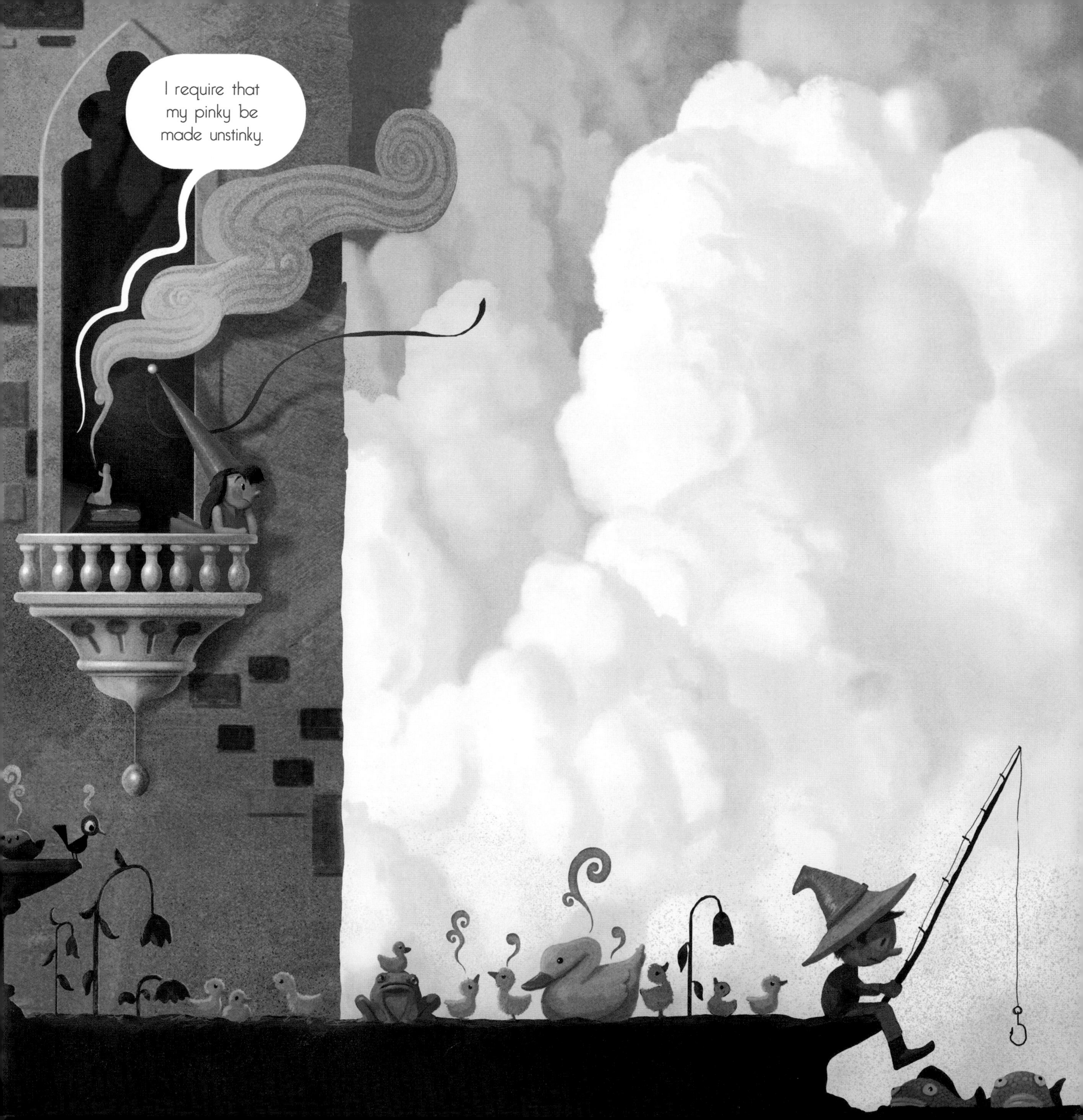
I require that my pinky be made unstinky.

Since there was no water to be had,

everyone in the kingdom

had to cry enough tears

so the king could wash

his pinky.

Now, this king's name was

King Blah Blah Blah,

and he had a daughter who was

Princess Blah Blah Blah,

and she was sooooo embarrassed

that her dad was making everyone

in the ENTIRE kingdom cry that she

went to the local old wizard guy and said . . .

The local old wizard guy did
some reading.

And some thinking.
And some drawing.
And math-ing.
And magicking.

And, you know . . . *things* started to happen.

"Hey, I'm a smallish magic bean," said the bean.

"Hey, I'm a smallish regular kid," said Jack.

"Well, let's do something big," suggested the bean.

"Okay," replied Jack.

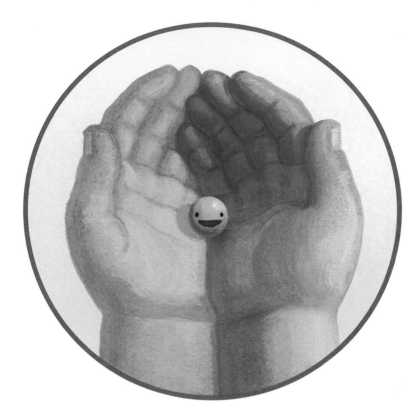

"All we need to do is dig a hole.

Put me in it.

Smooth the dirt.

Drip one drop of water
and repeat some magic words

three times,"

said the bean.

So . . . a hole was dug.

The bean was planted.

The dirt was smoothed.

A drip of water was dropped.

And Jack said,

"Give it a go.   Give it a go.   Give it a go."

And then things began . . . to . . .

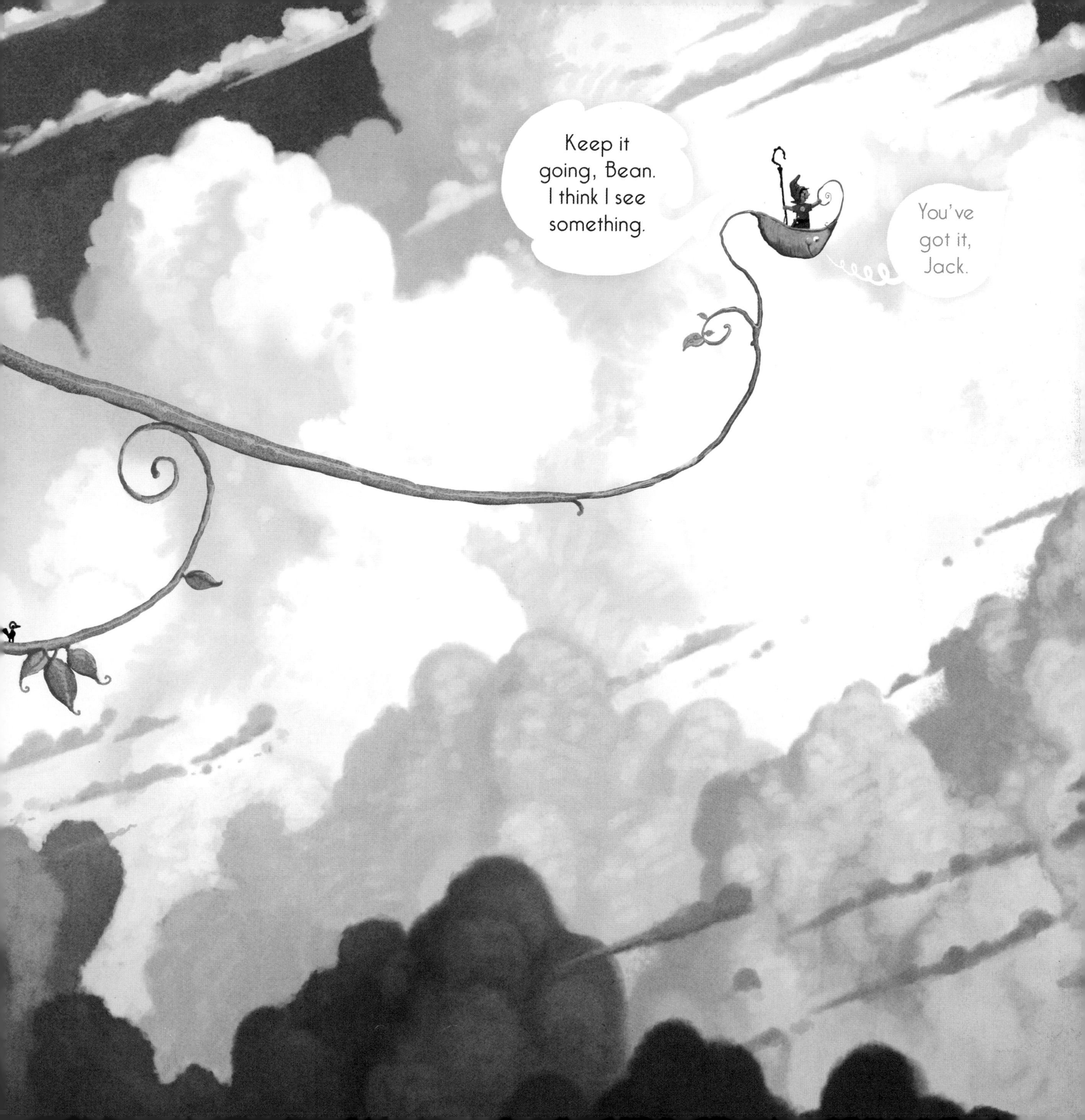
Keep it going, Bean. I think I see something.
You've got it, Jack.

GIANT house, Bean.
Big bubbles, Jack.
Gimme a little help, Bean.
All right-a-roonie, Jack.

The big bubbles were
coming from a really big bathtub
in which there sat . . .

guess who?

Hey, I'm a smallish giant kid named Don.
Hey, I'm a smallish regular kid named Jack.

"So, Don . . ."

"Yeah, Jack?"

"Been in the tub long?"

"Yeah. A loooong time. My pinky was stinky."

"Wow, that seems to be going around."

Suddenly, there was a giant

KNOCK KNOCK KNOCK

on the door.

"DON!"

"Yeah, Mom?"

"You've been in there forEVER!"

"Gee, Don, I guess you gotta go. . . ."

"Yeah . . ."

"But first lemme help you with that toe."

"It's funny what a big deal a little toe can be."

"Ya think, Jack?"

"Trust me, Don."

"And, Don?"

"Yeah, Jack?"

"Maybe turn off the faucet?"

"Good idea, Jack."

And then

Jack told Don good-bye

and rub-a-dub-dub-ed

his way home.

The trip was
a bit draining,
but then Jack found
his old pal.

Back at the castle,

the local old wizard guy announced

(with some satisfaction),

"Your Highness, may I present

a bean, a stalk and a boy named Jack."

And before the king could say

"Hey there, hi there, ho there,"

his pinky was unstinky.

"Whatta day," said the old wizard guy.

"Whatta bean," said Jack.

"Whatta boy," said the bean.

"I'm thirsty," said the bean.

"I'm Princess Blah Blah Blah," said
the princess. "But you can call me Jill."

"Well, Jill, wanna fetch a pail of water for my pal?" asked Jack.

"Sounds fun," said Jill.

And so . . .

they did.

The End . . . sorta.

To Carolyn and Billy Smith, who helped
a smallish boy grow up
—W. J.

To Candy and Steve Callicutt
—K. C.

MOONBOT books

Atheneum

ATHENEUM BOOKS FOR YOUNG READERS
An imprint of Simon & Schuster Children's Publishing Division
1230 Avenue of the Americas, New York, New York 10020
Copyright © 2014 by Moonbot Books
All rights reserved, including the right of reproduction in whole or in part in any form.
ATHENEUM BOOKS FOR YOUNG READERS is a registered trademark of Simon & Schuster, Inc.
Atheneum logo is a trademark of Simon & Schuster, Inc.
Moonbot and Moonbot Books are registered trademarks of Moonbot Studios LA LLC
For information about special discounts for bulk purchases, please contact Simon & Schuster Special Sales
at 1-866-506-1949 or business@simonandschuster.com.
The Simon & Schuster Speakers Bureau can bring authors to your live event. For more information or to book an event,
contact the Simon & Schuster Speakers Bureau at 1-866-248-3049 or visit our website at www.simonspeakers.com.
Book design by Moonbot Books and Ann Bobco
The text for this book is set in Aged Book.
The illustrations for this book are rendered in multimedia.
Manufactured in China
0714 SCP
First Edition
10 9 8 7 6 5 4 3 2 1
Library of Congress Cataloging-in-Publication Data
A bean, a stalk and a boy named Jack / Moonbot Studios. — First edition.
pages cm
Summary: A magic bean and an ordinary boy solve a royal problem for King Blah Blah Blah.
ISBN 978-1-4424-7349-2 (hardcover)
ISBN 978-1-4424-7350-8 (eBook)
[1. Fairy tales.] I. Moonbot Studios.
PZ8.B374 2015
[E]—dc23 2013041872